Beware of the
Neighbourhood Witch!

Mark Billen

Beware of the Neighbourhood Witch!

ISBN: 978-0-244-62945-8

Mark Billen is an accomplished playwright and his scripts have been highly praised because of their suitability for schools and youth drama groups. They have been performed in the United Kingdom and also in USA, Canada and Australia as well as in international schools in Ethiopia, Singapore, Sri Lanka, Switzerland, France and China.

A recent youth theatre play by Mark is *'Cinderella's Sisters – happy ever after?'* continuing the story of Clorinda and Tisbe after the wedding of their sister. The first production was given by Dreamaker Drama Academy, Beijing. Latest youth theatre plays by Mark are *'Beastly Baron Counterblast'* and *'All right! Snow White!'*

In 2015 Mark completed *'The Red King',* a satirical farce set in the future. This is Mark's first play intended for adults to perform.

Mark has also written a series of children's books for young readers featuring *Henry Bear and his Cousin Fred* together with their friends. These books are published in aid of the charity Action for Children.

Tales from The Forest and *When the gorse is in bloom …* are collections of short stories based on rural life in southern England.

Beware of the
Neighbourhood Witch

Chapter 1
The twin witches

Minnie and Gertie were twins. They were born within moments of each other but twins were never so different.

'Nobody likes you, Minnie,' said Gertie, 'because you're tall skinny and miserable. With all those tatty clothes and scuffed old boots you wear, you look like a dead stick.'

'Better to be like a dead stick than as short and as round and as jolly and as wobbly as a strawberry jelly,' said Minnie.

If you saw Minnie walking towards you then you would probably want to cross to the other side of the road as you would feel safer there. If you saw Gertie your face would break into a broad smile because she would be smiling as well. She always wore colourful clothes that cheered up even the dullest day. Minnie had sharp, bright, beady eyes that missed nothing but Gertie's eyes were kind, gentle and full of wisdom.

Gertie was always happy but her twin sister was only happy if she had something to grumble about. Minnie's face was always screwed up and looked as though she had just eaten something that tasted disgusting like a chocolate covered slug or a sugar coated wasp. Gertie's face was always full of smiles and jollity. She looked as if she had eaten something tasty like a lovely chocolate with a delicious creamy filling or a perfect bowl of peaches with lashings of her favourite ice cream.

There's something strange about Minnie. She is a witch and really she is a very bad witch. She is an extremely clever witch who can cast powerful spells that always work. Minnie waves a bony finger, mutters a few words and in a slice of a second the spell is cast. Minnie uses all of her magic spells to cause trouble. The more trouble she causes the happier Minnie becomes. If she is being nasty then Minnie is happy and the rest of the time she looks like the miserable haggard that she is.

There's something strange about Gertie as well. She is also a witch. Gertie is a very effective witch and her spells work very well too. The difference is that Gertie always uses her spells to help people and to make them happy. Her magic is just as effective as her twin sister's but the results are always very different.

If you had a problem with a blunt pencil Minnie would cast a spell that would make it look perfect but when you used it then there'd be a crack and it would break into pieces. But if Gertie made a spell to help you your pencil would last forever and never go blunt again.

How could twins be so different? That was something that really puzzled Gertie as she truly enjoyed life. The only thing that she didn't enjoy was being related to Minnie. 'But Minnie is my sister,' she would say to herself. 'She is part of my family.' Because of that Gertie would see Minnie once a week and hope that just once in a while her sister would actually be in a good mood.

Minnie thinks Gertie is crazy. She once said to her, 'What is the point of being a witch if you are going to be *nice* and *kind*? That's not being a proper witch! *Proper* witches work wicked spells and cause trouble, trouble, trouble! That's what real witches do! You're not a *real* witch. You should be doing simple conjuring tricks at children's parties, that's what you should be doing.'

'I'm perfectly happy doing things my own way,' Gertie replied. 'There's enough trouble about without me creating any more.'

'Don't be stupid!' screeched Minnie. 'It's not trouble, it's fun, fun, fun!'

'You have your type of fun and I shall have mine,' replied Gertie.

Minnie was so annoyed by Gertie's attitude that she did a very mean and horrible thing. Near Gertie's house was an orange and black round sign fixed to a lamppost that said 'Neighbourhood Watch'. Minnie saw this sign and mumbled to herself, 'I can do something to that sign! Oh yes I can!' and she gave a laugh that sounded like a frog gargling.

She began to mutter the spell.

'Itsy bitsy finger fine
Change the wording on this sign ...'

A small boy with red hair, bouncing a blue ball, was passing and he heard Minnie muttering away.

'What are you doing?' he asked. 'Are you talking to me?'

'I'm talking to myself!' snapped Minnie and she shot the boy such a nasty look that he felt as if an electric shock had passed through him, his red hair stood on end for a moment and he ran away. Because the spell had been interrupted she had to start again.

Minnie pointed her bony finger at the sign once more and stared at it with her sharp eyes.

'Itsy bitsy
Finger fine
Change the wording
On this sign
When my finger
Gives a twitch

It will say

'Neighbourhood Witch!'

Minnie twitched her gnarled finger at the 'Neighbourhood Watch' sign and for a moment it glowed brightly, flickered for a second or two and then settled down to its normal colours.

But there was a slight difference on the sign. Instead of a policeman's helmet the sign now showed a pointed witch's hat. And one letter had been changed. The 'a' in the word 'watch' had become a letter 'i'.

Minnie cackled quietly to herself. 'I wonder what will happen,' she thought, 'now everyone will see that there's a Neighbourhood Witch living close by!'

Chapter 2
Minnie's little tricks

One Thursday afternoon – Minnie and Gertie always met on Thursdays – Gertie needed to go shopping so she asked her sister to come with her. Gertie didn't really want to have Minnie with her but she was going to buy something heavy. She thought that she would need some help to carry the thing home.

Minnie was delighted to go shopping. She loved going shopping but usually didn't buy very much as she was too busy doing nasty things. Minnie liked shopping because normally she saw plenty of people about and that meant she could cause lots and lots of trouble. This made her feel very excited.

When they set off on the shopping expedition Gertie was surprised to see that Minnie looked happier than usual. In fact she was almost smiling and that made Gertie feel rather worried. She realised that her wicked sister had probably been making plans.

'You're looking happy today. Why are you looking so happy?'

'Ooooooh,' said Minnie as she quickly thought of an answer. She knew that if she told the truth Gertie would be angry. ' Ooooooh, … … er … I … I haven't been shopping for ages, that's why I'm feeling happy.'

Gertie was suspicious. She knew that if Minnie was happy then she was up to no good. Just then Gertie had a clever idea. She decided that she would try to walk just a step or two behind her sister. If Minnie did anything nasty or wicked then she would do her best to put it right.

As they walked to the bus stop Gertie passed the 'Neighbourhood Witch' sign. As the colours had not changed she didn't notice any difference. This irritated Minnie but she didn't dare to comment. She knew that Gertie would realise who had changed the sign. Minnie secretively thought, 'I'll make sure everyone sees that sign!'

The green and cream bus arrived and the twin witches climbed aboard.

'Where are off to today, ladies?' asked the cheerful round faced driver.

'Worchester, please,' said Gertie as she paid the fares.

He gave them their tickets and they settled into some seats towards the back of the bus. They behaved like any other ladies most of the time. However, Minnie couldn't control herself when she saw an old lady wearing a hat with decoration that looked like a bird. She secretively pointed a bony finger in the direction of the bird then waggled it. Immediately the bird began to stretch and flutter its wings. The old lady wearing the hat had no idea what was happening and Minnie began to giggle quietly. Even Gertie thought this was rather clever and she began to laugh as well.

'Ooh, Minnie, that is funny,' she whispered.

'Glad you like it,' answered Minnie. She waggled her finger again and the bird stopped moving.

'That's not nasty magic,' said Gertie. 'That's just a bit of fun.'

Eventually the bus stopped in Worchester and it was time for everyone to get off. Minnie waited until everyone else had left and then she walked to the door and Gertie followed.

As Minnie passed the driver's ticket machine she flicked a long bony finger on her right hand, and muttered,

'Itsy bitsy, gnats and crickets,
This machine will shoot out tickets!'

She cackled happily as the machine began to twirl out ticket after ticket in a great cascade of paper. Minnie was delighted as the machine just kept pushing out ticket after ticket after ticket after ticket after ticket after ticket!

The poor driver didn't know what to do. He stared at the machine thinking that it had gone crazy. He thumped it but that only seemed to make matters worse as the tickets came out faster than ever. Soon they were covering the floor and beginning to spew out of the bus and on to the pavement.

Gertie was furious. 'I'll sort this out!' she declared to herself and she pointed a meaty finger straight at the machine and mumbled,

'Itsy bitsy creak and crack,
Tickets now will all go back!'

There was a whirring, clatter of noise as the tickets slipped back into the machine. The long trail of tangled paper untangled itself, its knots unfolded as it slid its way back through the mouth shaped slot. Before long, there was nothing left on the floor of the bus.'

Just as the last few tickets were being swallowed into the machine Minnie turned round and saw what was happening. The machine stopped whirring and gave a loud click.

'Thank you for a lovely ride,' said Gertie as she clambered off the bus. She smiled sweetly at the driver who was looking dazed and amazed.

It was now Minnie's turn to be furious. 'What did you do that for?' she demanded. She said the words very crisply and spit shot out of her mouth as she spoke.

'You were causing trouble!' exclaimed Gertie. 'I don't think it's nice to cause trouble.'

'Dirty dog biscuits!' spat Minnie. 'It was fun. No one was hurt. Nobody was harmed. There wasn't any pain or suffering. I was just having a bit of fun. What's the point of being a witch if you can't have some fun?'

'Very well,' Gertie said but under her breath she added, 'If she wants some fun then I'll have some fun as well.'

The twin sisters began to walk to the shops. Suddenly Minnie began to giggle but it wasn't a nice giggle, it was a rather naughty giggle. She had seen the boy who had watched her when she changed the 'Neighbourhood Watch' sign. She recognised red hair and he was wearing the same blue shirt and red shorts. He was eating an ice cream that was in a cone. The boy had a great big smile on his face and he was clearly enjoying the delicious strawberry ice cream.

'I'll teach that scamp to spy on me!' thought Minnie. She stared at the ice cream and pointed at it, and then she began to twist her finger in circles.

> '*Hotsy totsy squirm and squeam,*
> *From the cone, jump out ice cream!*'

The ice cream seemed to lift itself out of the cone and up into the air. It climbed in a great curve and then it dropped with a splotty plop on to the dusty pavement. The little boy began to cry. Gertie saw a great big smile on Minnie's face and she knew what had happened.

'What's the matter, dear?' asked the little boy's mother.

'My … my ice cream,' wailed the little boy and tears began to show in his eyes.

Gertie lifted her finger and twisted it in reverse.

She pointed it at the ice cream and she quietly whispered,

'Hotsy totsy, squeam and squirm,
To the cone ice cream return!'

The ice cream lifted up off the pavement and back into the cone and it was as clean and fresh as it had been before Minnie's mean little spell. The little boy stopped crying and began to lick the lovely strawberry ice cream again. Gertie gave him a great big smile and he grinned back at her.

Minnie began to splutter. She was so cross that she could hardly let the words out of her mouth. In fact she was so hot with temper that when she did manage to speak little puffs of blue steam puffed from her nostrils because she was so angry. A few puffs even seeped from her ears!

'You! You! You! You stu … stu … stu … stupid interfering piece of pigeon's pecking!' she steamed and screamed. 'Mind your own business or I'll work a spell on you!'

'That's impossible,' answered Gertie calmly. 'We're twins and witches who are twins can't perform spells on each other because they just bounce back! You seem to have forgotten something'

'What's that?'

'Be careful! Remember, if you cast a spell on me I am your twin sister and so it will shoot back and hit you instead! Just remember that.'

Minnie gnashed her teeth when she heard this and even more blue steam came from her nostrils.

'Now let's stop arguing,' suggested Gertie. 'I've got to do some shopping.'

Gradually Minnie calmed down and she stopped breathing out steam as they walked along the pavement. Eventually they came to a large shop that sold all sorts of electrical items.

'Here's the shop I need,' declared Gertie. 'Now, promise me that you'll behave yourself,' she added.

'I promise that you won't see me doing anything wrong,' Minnie answered and then quietly giggled to herself because of the clever words that she had used. There was a curiously sly look on her face as well.

'That's good,' said Gertie as she went into the shop.

'What are you looking for?' asked Minnie who was suddenly sounding suspiciously nice.

'I need a new vacuum cleaner,' replied Gertie.

'Oooh, how exciting!' said Minnie, who still sounded far sweeter than usual. 'What a good idea! I've never used one of those things. I've always used my broomstick when I've wanted a ride. Do you think that one of these things will be comfortable to fly on?' she added.

'I don't think people use them to fly,' said Gertie. 'They are used for cleaning.'

'Well, that's amazing,' said Minnie. 'I don't think I'll buy one then. I'm not used to cleaning anything.'

Chapter 3
Shopping

Minnie and Gertie began looking at the different vacuum cleaners. There were so many that Gertie couldn't decide which one to choose. Should she have a red one or a maroon one? There were some nice blue ones and green ones. Some were upright so that you pushed them over the carpet. Others had cylinders with long hoses on to which nozzles and brushes and all sorts of exciting things could be attached.

Gertie and Minnie found all of this rather baffling but after a while a shop assistant came to talk to them.

'How can I help you, ladies?' asked the smart assistant.

'I'm thinking of buying a vacuum cleaner,' explained Gertie, 'but I really don't know much about them.'

'I'm sure that I can help you,' the assistant replied helpfully. He was soon having a long conversation with Gertie about vacuum cleaners and Minnie began to become bored, bored and even more bored.

Minnie decided to have a look at the other things for sale. First she went to look at the televisions. She liked them. She liked seeing the people on the screens. There was one man who was very smartly dressed in a grey suit and he seemed very serious so Minnie poked out her tongue at him and pulled her face in a funny way. The serious man didn't respond at all. Minnie was very disappointed so she decided to do something about it.

Remembering her promise Minnie looked to see where Gertie was. It was safe as Gertie was a long way off and was still discussing vacuum cleaners with the assistant. Minnie could keep her promise, as Gertie would never see what she did. Minnie pointed at the man on the television, wiggled her finger and whispered her spell:

'Crackle crickle, crickle crack
What I shall do, then you'll to back!'

Minnie stared at the man and he stared back at her. Then Minnie stroked her chin and the serious man stroked his chin.

'This is good,' thought Minnie, 'let's try something else!' She poked out her tongue as far as she could and the man on the television did exactly the same thing. He didn't look so serious now! There he was in his smart dark suit sticking his tongue out instead of talking on the news!

When Minnie looked around to see if anyone had noticed what she was doing she had a big surprise. There were rows of televisions on display and all of them were showing the same programme. Some had huge screens, some were smaller but on every television in full colour there was the same serious looking man poking his tongue out. Minnie gave an astonished gasp. She was thrilled, never before had her magic produced amazing, astonishing results.

Minnie thought this was wonderful and that she had been tremendously clever. She decided to try some more things. She again poked her tongue out as far as she could then put her hands by her ears and waggled them. The serious man on all of the television screens did exactly the same thing. Then Minnie decided to say some words as well.

'Oggle woggle poggle moggle foggle hoggle spoggle doggle!' said Minnie.

'Oggle woggle poggle moggle foggle hoggle spoggle doggle!' said the serious looking man on the television screens.

Minnie was hugely pleased with herself and felt so excited she began to bounce gently on the spot. Suddenly all of the television screens went blank and then a different man appeared and made an announcement.

'We seem to be having some technical problems,' he said, 'and so we are unable to continue our interview with the prime minister. Now here is the rest of the news.'

'Goodness gracious,' thought Minnie, 'what have I done?' She quickly moved away and decided to look at the washing machines.

In another part of the store Gertie and the assistant were getting on very well. Gertie had decided to have a round vacuum cleaner with a long hose. The only problem was that she couldn't decide whether to have a red one or a blue one.

Minnie saw that Gertie was still busy and so she decided there was time for more fun. She stood at the end of the rows of washing machines and tumble driers and quietly created a spell.

'Washing machines and tumble driers
In your rows from first to last
When I say 'biscuits' you'll spin fast!'

Nothing happened and that was just what Minnie expected, but if she said the word 'biscuits' the fun would begin. What's more, she knew exactly when she would say that word.

Gertie was paying the kind assistant for her vacuum cleaner. She had eventually decided that a red one would suit her best.

'Minnie, I've finished,' she called out. 'I need some help now.'

The vacuum cleaner was in a box that was far too heavy for her to carry on her own. Minnie came bustling over with a great big smile on her face.

'I've had a lovely time,' she said. 'This is such a fascinating place.'

'I'm glad you liked it,' said Gertie who was blissfully unaware of what had been going on.

'Let me help you with that box.'

There was a handle on each side so they were able to carry it quite easily.

Just as they were near the door Minnie said in a rather loud voice, 'Now I must buy myself some … er … *biscuits*!' She spoke the final word very clearly and a second later both of them were outside the shop.

Suddenly a great whirring sound began as every tumble drier and washing machine in the store magically switched itself on and began to spin. The spinning became faster and faster and louder and louder as all of the machines began to rumble and tumble, shudder and judder and bounce around in their rows.

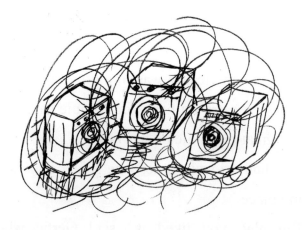

The lights on the machines gleamed and flashed. Red, green and orange lights flickered up and down the aisle as the machines uncontrollably set to work. All of the store assistants frantically dashed over to the machines and quickly began pressing every button on each machine.

Whatever they did made no difference as the machines just spun faster and faster and the whirring, humming sound grew louder and louder. Eventually the manager switched off all the electricity in the store and the machines settled down.

Gertie was so excited about having a new vacuum cleaner that she just kept talking. Minnie enjoyed hearing all of the noise coming from the store. She giggled softly and quietly chuckled to herself.

'I think we could make this load a bit lighter,' Minnie said to Gertie.

'That's a good idea,' said Gertie. 'Let's say it together.'

'Together,' agreed Minnie.

'Ibsy wibsy, obsy ware,
This big box shall float on air!'

After they had said the spell the heavy box floated along between them but they had to hold on tightly to make sure that it didn't float away. They just looked like two strangely different ladies carrying a large package. But then Minnie sneezed and let go of her end of the box!

'Are we going to the bus stop?' asked Minnie.

'I thought you wanted to buy some biscuits,' said Gertie.

'I'll leave them for today, I'm too tired,' said Minnie. 'Let's catch the bus home.'

They walked to the bus stop and for once Minnie behaved herself. When the bus arrived Gertie was pleased to see that the driver had a thin face and grey hair. He was not the man they had seen earlier in the day. They showed their return tickets, floated the box on to the bus and put it safely on the rack. Gertie gave the box a firm tap and it settled down and stopped floating. Minnie and Gertie made themselves comfortable on a seat nearby.

'I'd never have one of those things,' Minnie declared. 'What's the point in cleaning everywhere when it will soon be dirty again?'

'A vacuum cleaner can be very useful if you use it properly,' answered Gertie.

'What do you mean by that?' asked Minnie. 'It's just a dull vacuum cleaner.'

'I'll find plenty of uses for it,' said Gertie, 'as well as cleaning.'

'I don't know what you mean!' snapped Minnie and she wouldn't talk for the rest of the journey.

When it was time to get off the bus Minnie and Gertie tapped the box together and it floated between from the bus, on to the pavement and they walked with it to Gertie's house.

Once again they passed the 'Neighbourhood Witch' sign but Gertie didn't notice it. Minnie was in a bad mood so she wouldn't chat but her twin sister didn't mind. If Minnie was silent at least she wasn't arguing about anything.

Chapter 4
Teatime

Minnie and Gertie walked from the bus stop to Gertie's house. As soon as they were in Gertie's cosy, comfortable house Minnie could smell that a home-made cake had been baked and Minnie loved Gertie's cakes. For a moment Minnie was in a good mood and she flopped into an armchair and put her feet up on a coffee table.

She was actually rather tired after using so much magic in one afternoon. Maria, Gertie's white cat, suddenly appeared and jumped up on to Minnie's lap.

'Get off me!' shrieked Minnie. 'You're not a witch's cat. Witches should have black cats.' Maria stared hard at Minnie then jumped off her lap and slowly left the room. Maria had decided that she did not like Minnie and her stately steps made this perfectly clear. As she went through the door Maria gave Minnie a very meaningful stare and then walked off.

'I don't know why you keep that moggie,' muttered Minnie to herself. 'She's about as much use as hole in a crumpet.'

Gertie did not hear Minnie's mutterings as she was in her kitchen.

'Make me a nice cup of tea, Gertie!' she demanded. Gertie was feeling in a happy mood as she thought Minnie had been very helpful and she hadn't been too much trouble.

'Certainly, Minnie,' said Gertie with a happy smile. 'I'll cut us some fruit cake as well. I made it this morning.'

'Good,' said Minnie, 'cut me a large slice! And wipe that smile of your face! Why do you have to look so happy all of the time?'

Gertie didn't bother to answer Minnie but made the tea and cut the cake.

'Move your feet off the table, Minnie, or we'll have a fine mess everywhere.'

'Suppose I could,' grumbled Minnie and she moved a stool near and put her feet up on that. 'Make sure my tea's nice and strong. I don't want any weak and watery stuff. Three sugars in it and I'll have a big slice of cake,' she added.

'Try saying please,' suggested Gertie.

'Please yourself!' Minnie snapped rudely. 'Just give me the tea and cake.'

Gertie poured the tea and passed the cake. Minnie just grabbed the cup and saucer and began drinking noisily making horrible spluttering sounds.

She gobbled a chunk of the cake and sat chewing it for some time because she had shoved too much into her mouth. As soon as she could Minnie took a gulp of tea to try and wash the cake down. She really was being quite disgusting. A moment later she gave a great rumbling belch that made the curtains flutter.By this time it was nearly six o'clock. Gertie decided she would like to watch the television, so she switched it on.

'We'll be just in time for the news,' said Gertie.

'Suit yourself!' snapped Minnie as she grabbed another piece of fruitcake and began stuffing it into her mouth and slurping more tea. 'I never watch the news. There's never anything interesting on the news.'

The news began and Gertie watched whilst Minnie tried to ignore the television altogether. 'A strange electrical fault has occurred causing unusual problems in the Worchester area. During an interview the prime minister suddenly responded in a strange way. He poked his tongue out in a rude manner and in response to a question replied, 'Oggle woggle poggle moggle foggle hoggle spoggle doggle!' A few minutes later all of the washing machines and tumble driers in an electrical store began to spin at once. They could not be stopped until the mains supply had been switched off. It is believed that an electrical fault at the store was the source of both problems. Brendan Carter reports from the store. Do you have any more news for us Brendan?'

Both Gertie and Minnie were paying full attention but Minnie was pretending that she wasn't interested. Suddenly the picture changed to somewhere they both recognised. The reporter was standing outside the store where they had been earlier in the afternoon.

'There certainly has been something strange here today,' declared Brendan Carter. 'It seems that there was a peculiar type of electrical interference that affected this area and spread through the wires to other places. At this moment no one is sure exactly ...'

'What have you been up to, Minnie?' demanded Gertie.

'What? What?' asked Minnie who was still trying to look as though she wasn't interested in the news.

'You know what I mean! You promised me that you would behave yourself!'

'Oh no I didn't! I promised that you wouldn't *see* me doing anything wrong. That's different! I just had some fun. I didn't break my promise.'

'So it *was* you! You caused all that trouble! It's not safe to take you anywhere!'

'Pinkie - pigs - tails to you!' exclaimed Minnie and then she gave another booming, big belchy burp because she had guzzled the tea and cake far too quickly. 'Stop being such a bossy boots goody, goody Gertie! I'll do what I want to and a goody, goody like you isn't going to stop me!' She stood up and strode to the door.

'Bad-bye!' she shouted and she whisked out through the door into the hall and through the front door in one big dramatic sweep.

'Oh dear,' said Gertie to herself. 'It's usually the same. We end up having an argument. It's such a shame that we can't enjoy being with each other.' Gertie felt rather sad that the afternoon had ended in such an unpleasant way. 'But she is my sister. My twin sister,' she quietly said to herself.

After Minnie had stormed out of Gertie's home her temper did not improve. Really it couldn't improve because she was in a foul and mean mood and that meant that all she wanted to do was something horrible to anyone she encountered.

She saw a postman about to empty a letterbox and her mind raced. What could she do that would be fun? Something hilarious … something surprising? As the postman approached the letter box Minnie whispered,

'Letterbox with letters in it
Now you can talk for just a minute.'

By now the postman had reached into his pocket for his keys. As he was about to put the key in the keyhole a voice that seemed to be in the box said, 'At last you've come!'

'What … what was that?'

'What sort of time do you call this? You're late and we've been stuck in here all this time.'

'Who … who .. is there? Where are you?'

'Open the box and letters out.'

'Let who out?'

'No! Letters out! Open the box!'

'Must I? M … must I? I don't know what to do!'

'Come on, letters out! We're all squashed up in here! We're sitting on top of each other!'

Minnie was shaking with gleeful laughter but now the minute was over and she knew nothing more would happen. Shivering in fear the postman opened the box but all he found was a perfectly normal pile of letters. He hastily swept them in to his sack, slammed the door of the box and locked it. He then climbed on to his bike and pedalled away so fast that his legs were barely visible.

'That's made me feel better,' Minnie muttered to herself, but a moment later he mood grew worse. She looked up and saw the 'Neighbourhood Witch' that Gertie hadn't even noticed. 'I'll get it noticed!' she said. Her bony finger pointed at the sign and she breathily created another spell.

'*Warning sign you have to show*
A witch is near so people know
Therefore as the night comes dark
In the gloom you'll glow and spark!'

The sun was just setting as Minnie said this so she decided to wait a few minutes to see the effect of her spell.

Not wanting to be too obvious in case people mistook her for the witch Minnie decided to hide in some bushes as the evening sky darkened. This turned out to be a mistake as a large brown dog was also in the bushes and it had a very meaty bone. The dog thought Minnie was after his bone so he snarled and growled making Minnie shake and quiver from top to toe. The snarls became deeper and more menacing and Minnie dashed from the bush straight into the stomach of a passing policeman.

'Oof! Ouch!' groaned the policeman.

The snarls of the dog grew louder.

'Dog … d … dog!' gasped Minnie pointing into the bushes. 'Big … big … dog!'

The policeman dashed into the bushes to investigate the menacing noises. Minnie took her chance to rush away from the scene. The sign that was now glowing and flashing very brightly.

Chapter 5
The vacuum cleaner

Gertie switched her television off and to take her mind off the bad time with Minnie she decided to open the box that held her new, red vacuum cleaner. She soon had it open and she became very excited by all the things that came with it. As well as a long black hose there were some black tubes, a useful nozzle to get into difficult places and a variety of brushes for cleaning different things. Gertie found everything very interesting and she settled down to read the instruction book. Whilst she was reading Maria strolled back into the room and settled herself comfortably in an armchair where she purred contentedly.

Although she felt rather tired Gertie thought it would be fun to test the new machine. She attached the black hose and two of the tubes. On the end of one of the tubes she added a brush then she plugged the machine in and switched it on.

As soon as the machine was switched on an exciting whirring noise began. The black hose together with the tubes and the brushes began to stand up and twist around the room as if they had come alive. Gertie stared in astonishment as the brush came towards her waving to the left and the right. Then the brush swung around and headed towards Maria who shrank back in the chair as it came closer.

Gertie stared at the brush then dashed to the machine and switched it off. Immediately the brush and tubes settled down on the carpet.

'Phew!' said Gertie and she sat down for a few minutes and flapped her hand to cool down after the excitement.

She sat thinking for a moment. 'I can do a lot of things with this machine,' she said quietly to herself.

'Maria, this machine will be very useful for all sorts of things especially when I am in control.'

Maria didn't say anything but she stared at Gertie then nodded her head.

'You think so, as well,' said Gertie. 'You agree because you are a clever cat and you understand everything that I say.' Maria snuggled back into the chair and began to purr again and then she went to sleep.'

The next morning Gertie woke up feeling very excited as she was going to test the new vacuum cleaner. Gertie wanted to find out what she could do with it! First of all she did some ordinary cleaning and sucked up the mud that had dropped from Minnie's shoes and all the crumbs that had fallen on to the carpet whilst she had been greedily stuffing cake into her mouth. Throughout all this activity Maria, Gertie's white cat, sat very still and watched every move that Gertie made. Maria was not quite sure what to think about this machine.

Gertie picked up Maria. The cat immediately became very stiff and suspicious. Gertie pressed a different button on the cleaner and suddenly the whirr changed to a gentle hum and the machine just sucked gently. Gertie brushed over Maria's fur with the vacuum cleaner and the cat began to purr.

'You like that, don't you?' Gertie said to her cat and Maria purred even more. 'I made it especially gentle just for you! Only my vacuum cleaner is suitable for cats so don't get in the way of other vacuum cleaners.' Maria purred and nodded her head in agreement.

It was a rather windy day and Mrs Dawkins, who lived next door to Gertie, was doing her washing. Whilst she was trying to peg the washing on the clothesline to dry there were some strong gusts of wind. The wind tugged at the washing on the line loosening the clothes pegs. Suddenly two shirts, a blouse, two pairs of trousers and three hankies were tugged from the line and they went sailing into the air.

The wind twirled them and whirled them round the garden and Mrs Dawkins began to shriek in astonishment.

Gertie saw the clothes whirling about and realised what had happened. She flung open the window and

pushed the nozzle of the vacuum cleaner outside and
pointed it at the clothes.

'Ooper booper super strong,

Stop those shirts from taking flight,

Ooper booper super long,

Fetch the blouse and hold on tight.

Ooper booper nothing's wrong

Bring those trousers to the ground

Ooper booper don't be long

Stop those hankies whirling round!'

Whilst Gertie spoke the rhyme the long hose on the vacuum cleaner snaked through the window and stretched it self over the gardens. The vacuum cleaner began to whirr with super speed and amazing things started to happen.

First it chased the shirts and sucked hard upon them and brought them down to Mrs Dawkins who was standing with her mouth open and her hair flying backwards in the wind. The hose snaked up and away, rescued the blouse and took it to Mrs Dawkins. Without waiting it then chased after the trousers. One pair was easily saved as it was caught in a tree but the other pair was blowing all over the garden. The hose twisted and turned, rose up into the air and then dived down again.

'Naughty trousers you'll be caught,
And a lesson you'll be taught!'

Suddenly the hose caught the trousers, brought them down, put them on the ground and then smacked them hard five times! When it had done that the hose flew away and chased after the hankies. They were easily caught, as they had not gone far. As soon as all the washing was back with Mrs Dawkins the black hose shrunk back to its normal size, the mighty whirring slowed down and the vacuum cleaner even switched itself off.

'Goodness gracious!' exclaimed Gertie. 'Well I never did … Would you believe it?'

Gertie sat flapping herself with her hand to cool herself down as she was almost as astonished as Mrs Dawkins. Gradually she calmed down, cooled off and sat staring at the vacuum cleaner. After a moment Maria came and inspected it very carefully.

'What else can this amazing machine do?' Gertie said to herself. She couldn't think of anything else that she wanted it to do other than normal house work but she was sure that sooner or later the vacuum cleaner would do some more astonishing things.

Gertie was just thinking about making some tea when she saw that a policeman was walking up her garden path. 'That's odd,' she thought. 'I wonder what's wrong? Why is Bert Hoggings coming to see me?' Because Gertie was such a jolly and friendly person she knew almost everyone in the neighbourhood.

'Good morning, Bert,' said Gertie as she opened the front door. 'What can I do for you?'

'There's something nasty going on, very nasty.'

'What's that?'

'Someone has changed the sign outside your house,' said Bert. 'It now says 'Neighbourhood Witch' instead of 'Neighbourhood Watch'.

Then Gertie did the last thing Bert expected. She burst into laughter. 'Does it really? How funny!' And Gertie could not stop chuckling to herself.

'And that's not nice. A sign like that could frighten children.'

'I agree, I wonder who changed it,' she added, knowing perfectly well who was responsible.

'Someone nasty, with a cruel sense of humour.'

'Now then Bert, stop worrying and stay and have a cup of tea,' said Gertie and I'll get that sign sorted out for you.

Bert sat himself down, nearly filling an armchair, and Gertie went into the kitchen. She set the kettle to boil then opened a window so that she could just see the sign. There it was gleaming in orange and black with the letter A in 'watch' replaced with I and a witch's black hat instead of a policeman's helmet.

'Right, Minnie, I'll soon sort this out!' she muttered.

She made sure the kitchen door was shut for a moment then pointing at the sign she whispered;

'When my fingers give a twitch
Sign read 'watch' instead of 'witch'
A helmet will replace that hat
That is right and that is that!'

Gertie made her fingers do a peculiar twisting motion in the direction of the sign. At first nothing seemed to happen but gradually the warning sign began to turn then it spun rapidly like a Catherine Wheel before settling back into place.

Gertie finished making the tea and took it into the sitting room where Bert was sprawled on a sofa with his eyes closed and soft snores were coming from his open mouth.

'Needn't have worried,' muttered Gertie. 'Here's the tea Bert!' she added in a much louder voice. He woke up and they were soon chatting about normal things.

'Well, better be on my way,' said Bert, 'nice to see you, Gertie. I hope that silly sign hasn't upset you.'

'Not at all, it's quite funny really. I'm sure I can sort it out'

'Well, I'll be off then.' Policeman Bert walked out of the cottage and along the garden path. As he went through the gate he looked up at the sign.

'Neighbourhood Watch!' he said. 'And a proper helmet... have I been imagining things? Better not talk about this.'

Minnie's 'little joke' did not upset Gertie and she was not in the least surprised by it. However, it did have one effect on her. She became very determined that Minnie was not going to upset her anymore and if Minnie got herself into trouble ... well Minnie must sort out her problems for herself. Gertie also decided that Minnie must be taught a lesson but she wasn't sure what she might do

Chapter 6
The birthday

The next day began bright and sunny. Gertie remembered that it was little Ricky's birthday. Ricky was Mrs Dawkins little boy and Gertie wanted to give him a birthday present. The present was already wrapped in red paper with a great big yellow ribbon tied round it.

'I'm just popping next door,' Gertie said to Maria, but the cat didn't take any notice, as she was asleep in the chair. Gertie had a big smile on her face, as she was sure Ricky would like the present.

Gertie knocked at the door, Mrs Dawkins opened it and Ricky peered round her skirts. When he saw Gertie he grinned happily.

'Happy Birthday, Ricky!' exclaimed Gertie. 'I hope you have a lovely day.

'Come in Gertie,' said Ricky's mum, 'it's nice to see you.'

'I've come to give Ricky his birthday present,' explained Gertie and Ricky giggled.

'I'll make a pot of tea.' Mrs Dawkins went off to the kitchen and Gertie was happy to be with Ricky in the sitting room.

'How old are you today, Ricky?'

'Four!'

'Well, here's a present for you!' and Gertie gave Ricky the parcel. He sat down on the floor and tried to open it, but Gertie had tied it up too well and whatever Ricky did he could not undo the yellow ribbon.

'I can't open it!' Ricky declared as he struggled.

'Oh, dear,' said Gertie and pointing her finger at the parcel she whispered a simple spell.

'Bow undo, untwist, untie,
Knots untangle, you know why!
Paper, unfold, do not be tricky,
Parcel open up for Ricky!'

Immediately the ribbon bow started to undo, then it seemed to struggle for a moment, as the knot was untangled. Suddenly the ribbon was loose. Ricky looked in astonishment but did not know what to say. Next there was a rustling sound as the paper unfolded and took itself away from the present.

'Oooh!' said Ricky as he saw a red and blue toy lorry that looked extremely real but very small. The lorry looked even more realistic a moment later, after Gertie had pointed a finger at it and said,

> *'Roundy - roundy, wheels turn round*
> *Lorry move along the ground*
> *Roundy – roundy don't be tricky*
> *Drive everywhere for Master Ricky!'*

As soon as Gertie had said these words the little lorry began to drive around the room. It never bumped in to anything. It would stop, reverse, turn round and then move off again.

'Ooh! Ooh!' said Ricky and his mouth was wide open in amazement.

Ricky loaded the lorry with bricks and then the lorry moved off and carried the bricks to another part of the room. He was fascinated. He unloaded the bricks and began to build a little shed for the lorry.

'What a wonderful present,' said Ricky's mother as she came in to the room carrying a tray with two mugs of tea and an orange juice. 'I've never seen a lorry like that before.'

'It's new,' explained Gertie, 'It's the first one I've seen.'

'Thank you very much,' said Ricky. 'It's wonderful.'

'What's happening today?' asked Gertie, who preferred not to talk about the lorry.

'I'm having a party in the garden.'

'And a conjuror as well,' added Mrs Dawkins.

'Well, I hope you have a wonderful time,' said Gertie as she sipped her tea.

Ricky played with his new lorry as the two ladies chatted and then Gertie decided it was time to go. As she left Ricky waved goodbye then suddenly burst in to tears as he stood on the doorstep.

'What's the matter, Ricky?' asked Gertie.

'Look!' cried Ricky as he pointed up at the sky. The sun had disappeared and dark grey clouds were building up. 'It will rain and I won't be able to have my party.'

'You never know with the weather,' Gertie said soothingly, 'it will probably clear up before this afternoon.'

Gertie returned to her house and brought out her vacuum cleaner. She connected it up and then opened the window so that she could point the long black hose up to the clouds.

'Now for some really tough magic,' Gertie muttered to the vacuum cleaner. 'This will test your magical power and mine!' She stood with her eyes closed and concentrated on what she had to do and then she suddenly switched on the machine and spoke using a very firm voice.

'Vacuum cleaner, super strong,
Stretch your black hose, extra long!
Reach the clouds that hover here,
Suck them away, the sky make clear!'

The vacuum cleaner's humming became stronger and deeper and the vacuum hose grew and grew as it climbed up and up above Gertie's house.

It slowly stretched and squirmed and stretched up above the trees higher and higher and up into the clouds.

'Now vacuum cleaner,
Super power
Will stop the clouds
That cause a shower!
Don't be feeble, be most strong!
Use that power with hose so long!'

'Whirrrrrrrrrrr!' went the vacuum cleaner and there seemed to be another great surge of power. Looking up to the clouds Gertie watched as a big, grim, slgrey cloud began to be sucked in by the hose of vacuum cleaner. At first it was just a long, puffy, grey finger that was pulled in by the hose but then the rest of the cloud followed. It twisted and turned as if it was struggling but the more it moved the stronger the power of the vacuum cleaner became and gradually the cloud was sucked from the sky.

There was a very dark cloud looming overhead. The hose stretched out to it. This was a fat and lazy cloud that didn't bother to struggle but the cleaner had to work hard because there was so much of it. Gradually it too was sucked from the sky. More grim clouds were gradually sucked down from the sky and squeezed into the nozzle of the vacuum cleaner and the day became brighter. Soon the only clouds left behind were just puffy white clouds that floated around harmlessly. The sun was shining brightly again and soon even the puffy white clouds had given up and disappeared.

Feeling she had done some good work Gertie switched off the vacuum cleaner and put it away. As the window was still open she could hear Ricky and his mother in their garden. Ricky sounded very happy. Gertie went to see him.

'I told you that the weather often changes,' she said to Ricky.

'We'll have a lovely time now,' said his mother. A telephone began to ring and Mrs Dawkins dashed in to the house. Gertie stayed chatting to Ricky.

'What sort of food are you having at your party, Ricky?' she asked.

'Sausages, chocolate biscuits, ice cream, jelly ... I can't remember everything.'

'I expect you'll be having a cake.'

'Yes, mummy's made a lovely cake,' he said.

Mrs Dawkins reappeared looking very worried. 'The conjuror can't come, he's ill, I don't know what to do,' she said and she looked very worried.

'I'll come and help you,' said Gertie before Ricky could begin to cry. 'I know a few tricks that will make everyone happy!'

'Really, are you sure? Oh that would be amazing! We start at four o'clock if that's okay?' said Mrs Dawkins.

'Leave it to me,' said Gertie. 'I'll be there!'

It was several days since Minnie and Gertie had gone shopping. Minnie couldn't stop thinking about Gertie. She rather missed seeing her even though they were so different. She didn't want Gertie to realise how she felt so she decided to disguise herself.

Minnie used her magical powers quite often and usually to do things that she should have been ashamed of. She loved causing chaos by turning all the traffic lights to red and watching as the whole town came to a standstill. She thought it was tremendous fun to make all the church bells start ringing in the middle of the night so that everyone for miles was wide awake when they wanted to be asleep

When Minnie saw that her magic on the 'Neighbourhood Watch' sign had been reversed she was furious. She was so angry that her face became pink, then orange, began to glow and eventually was as red as an over-ripe tomato. She stood in front of the sign muttering nasty words that so astonished a passing black cat that it shot to the other side of the road and sat on top of a post box staring at Minnie.

'Cat! Who are you staring at?' snapped the angry witch.

The cat just stayed where it was watching Minnie with great care.

Minnie tried to ignore the cat and turned her attention to the sign.

'I'll work some new magic,' she said to herself. 'Some new magic so my stupid sister won't be able to change what I have done!'

The cat continued to stare intensely at Minnie with sharp piercing green eyes. She turned away from the cat but every now and then could not resist glancing back. The cat continued to watch Minnie's every move.

'Hmmm,' muttered Minnie to herself. 'Stop being silly, Minnie. Stop fussing about a nosey cat!'

She gradually prepared herself for making a spell and concentrated her mind and pointed at the sign two tight fingers.

'Sign so bright that's in my range,
After this you'll never change,

Minnie did not see that the cat had jumped from the post box, and was now sitting right beside her staring and listening very carefully.

After my fingers give this twitch
*You'll **always** read*
'Neighbourhood Witch!'

Then Minnie twitched and clicked her two fingers and the sign seemed to crackle for a moment.

Minnie looked down and saw the cat watching her. She really did not like those piercing green eyes.

'What are you up to?' demanded Minnie. 'Tell me!'

The cat continued to stare.

'What's the matter? Cat got your tongue?' snapped Minnie, then realising what a stupid comment she had made she strode away. The cat gently wandered off wondering what this peculiar woman was up to.

When Minnie reached her garden gate she was relieved to find that the cat had not followed her. Minnie's home had a wonky roof with tiles trying to fall off and creepers growing over the windows. The chimney looked as if it might collapse at any moment. She went into her tumbledown house and sat down on a big chair. This disturbed a lot of dust as Minnie never cleaned anything. A moment later she gave a very loud sneeze that disturbed even more dust which caused her to sneeze seven more times. Once the dust had settled Minnie's sneezing stopped and she began to think.

Minnie was wondering what she could do to outwit her goody, goody sister. She wanted to know more about her. What could she do …? Minnie sat pondering and thinking until her brain was so tired that she went to sleep. Minnie's brain had continued working whilst she dozed and she suddenly woke up with a start as a brilliant idea had shot into her mind.

The brilliant idea was to use her magical powers in a different way. She would do something useful for a change. Something really useful for one person – Minnie! She decided to turn herself into a bird then she would be able to fly to Gertie's house and see what she was up to. Gertie would never know that she was being watched!

Minnie stood very still and began to chant the spell.

'Oogle boogle! Magic grow!
Turn myself into a crow!
Turn my dress to feathers black!
Give me wings upon my back!
Feet become claws of a bird
So I'll look real and not absurd!

Minnie had scarcely finished casting the spell when she felt herself beginning to shrink and she felt her arms flapping in a peculiar way. It was a very peculiar feeling! She looked down and her feet and saw that she had claws.

Minnie felt immensely pleased with how her clever scheme was working. She flapped her wings and in a moment was nearly hitting the ceiling of her home. That was exciting – she really could fly like a bird.

'I am so clever! I can fly without a broomstick!'

She flew out through the open window into the garden and landed on the grass. She thought that flying like this was rather fun and so she practised a few times and then decided it was time for her to go and see what Minnie was up to.

Chapter 7
The Party

By now it was four o'clock and the sun was shining brightly. Ricky's birthday party was going very well. All his friends had arrived and were playing in the garden.

Gertie was prepared do her special tricks and she was going to put on a real magic show. She put out on a table a large bowl and a long wooden spoon.

Ricky's mother called Ricky's friends and they all sat on rugs watching as Gertie began telling a story.

'I want to make a cake for you this afternoon. So I need you to help me. First of all I need an egg. Has anyone brought an egg to the party.'

'No,' chorused all the children. A little girl suddenly began to make funny clucking noises.

'Cluckety – cluckety – cluck.'

'What's wrong, dear?' asked Gertie.

'Cluck – cluckety – cluck.'

The little girl began to wriggle and fidget and suddenly she stood up and found that she had been sitting on an egg! The little girl laughed.

'I knew someone here had an egg!' declared Gertie. 'What's your name dear?'

'Amy,' said the little girl.

'Well, thank you for the egg, Amy,' said Gertie. 'Now I need some flour, but I haven't brought any. What ever shall I do?'

The children called out all sorts of ideas.

'Use some soil!'

'Sand would do.'

'Why not some flowers?'

'That's a good idea,' said Gertie, 'Could you all pick some daisies as the flour must be white?'

The children began picking daisies from the lawn and they brought them to Gertie.

As they were doing this a black crow with sharp, bright beady eyes flew in to the garden and settled on the fence. It sat there and watched everything that Gertie was doing and every now and then the crow's head bobbed up and down and it cackled to itself. The children gave all of

the white daisies to Gertie and she put them into a big
bowl.

'I need another egg,' said Gertie and immediately
another child began to wriggle. 'What's wrong with you?'
asked Gertie.

'Cluckety - cluck! There's something … cluck -
cluckety … under me,' said the boy and he wriggled even
more then jumped up. 'I was sitting on an egg! Who put
that there?'

'I've no idea,' said Gertie and as she spoke the
crow gave another cackling laugh.

'Now I need some dates. Where can I find some
dates?' None of the children had any ideas. 'I'll use a

newspaper! There's always dates at the top of a newspaper!' Gertie put her hand up in the air and a newspaper appeared. She tore off the dates from the top of the page and put them in the bowl. 'There you, there's some nice dates.' The children all giggled.

'Has anyone brought some butter?' asked Gertie, 'I must have some butter.'

'Use buttercups!' called out a girl and the children picked buttercups and Gertie added them to the bowl.

'I think we've found everything now. Let's mix everything up and make the cake.' Gertie produced the wooden spoon. 'Who's going to help me stir the cake?'

'I will!' said Ricky and he began mixing up the eggs, the dates the daisies and the buttercups.

The crow watched everything and then cackled again, but this time there were some words in the cackle and Gertie knew what those words were. The children didn't hear the words, as they were busy stirring the cake.

'Conjuring tricks!' cackled the crow. 'You're doing conjuring tricks at a children's party! Witches don't do things like that!' Having cackled these comments the crow flew away squawking more rude remarks as it flew

'Let's bake the cake,' said Gertie as she tipped the revolting mixture into a baking tin.

'Ugh!' groaned all the children as they saw the revolting mixture slide out of the bowl. 'Ugh!'

'That looks lovely,' said Gertie, 'I'm sure we'll have a beautiful cake. How shall we cook it? I need an oven. Has anyone brought an oven with them?'

'No!' said all the children.

'Oh dear, we've got to cook it somehow. Did *nobody* bring an oven with them?'

The children all giggled and chorused, 'No!' together and then giggled some more.

'Well, I brought an oven,' said Gertie. 'Here it is!' Gertie held out her empty hands and turned round so that children could only see the back of her. She didn't stop but kept on turning and when she was facing the children again she was holding an oven. The children all sat in silence with their mouths open.

'What's the matter? Haven't you seen an oven before?' The children remained silent. 'Come on Ricky, it's your birthday so you must put the cake in the oven.'

Gertie opened the oven door and Ricky popped the cake tin in the oven. Gertie shut the door firmly.

'We need to time the cooking,' she said, 'so I need a clock! What are you sitting on Amy?' asked Gertie.

'A rug!' said Amy, but then she started to fidget and fidget.

'Stand up, dear,' said Gertie and Amy stood up and then bent down and picked up a clock.

'I knew one of you would have a clock,' said Gertie, 'now how long will the cake take to cook?'

The children called out all sorts of times but eventually everyone agreed that it would need about forty minutes.

'That means it will be ready at five o'clock,' said Gertie. 'We can't wait that long! I'll change the clock.' She tapped the clock and the hands twirled round until it said that it was five o'clock. 'There, the cake's cooked!' Gertie declared.

'It can't be!' said one child.

'Oh yes it can!' Gertie answered.

'Oh no it can't' chorused the children.

'Oh yes it can!' This went on for some time and the children became more and more excited and bounced up and down.

'Yes it can!' Gertie said very quickly.

'No it can't!' all the children chorused just as fast.

Gertie held up her hand and they fell silent. 'There's only one way to find out,' declared Gertie. 'Open the oven Ricky!'

Ricky went to the oven and opened it and Gertie used an oven glove to take the hot cake from the oven. Suddenly a delicious smell spread over the garden and the children all went, 'Oooh!'

At that moment the crow flew over the garden again. 'Conjuring tricks!' it squawked. 'Conjuring tricks! You're just the Neighbourhood Witch!

Chapter 8

Super, super vacuum cleaner

The children had enjoyed themselves tremendously and so had Gertie but when the party was over she felt tired. She went home and settled down with a cup of tea. Maria came in through the open window and settled on Gertie's lap and purred contentedly. Gertie stroked her cat, relaxed and drifted off to sleep.

'Conjuring tricks!' squawked the crow. It had flown to the open window and was sitting on the sill. 'Conjuring tricks!'

Gertie woke with a start and Maria jumped off her lap. 'Be quiet Minnie!' said Gertie. 'I know it's you. You may look like a bird but you still have sharp, bright beady eyes!'

'Yes, it's me. Don't you think I'm clever turning myself into a crow? That's better than conjuring tricks.'

'You are very clever, Minnie. I hope you like being a crow.'

'Awk! It's great fun. I can fly anywhere very quickly and I can see what you are up to.'

'You haven't seen my vacuum cleaner, have you?' said Gertie. An idea was taking shape in her mind.

'Stinky –winky! I don't want to see the useless thing.'

'It does wonderful things,' said Gertie as she took it out of the cupboard and plugged it in. 'I've found it very useful.'

'Blue bananas! I don't care what it does! Won't make any difference to me! You're just the Neighbourhood Witch!' she croaked.

Gertie's idea was becoming stronger and stronger. It was not the type of idea that Gertie usually had but she was rather tired and she was feeling that she had put up with too many of Minnie's rude remarks and crazy magic. Gertie knew that she couldn't cast a spell upon Minnie as it would bounce back and hit her instead. That's what happens with twins who are witches. But Gertie realised there was something she could do with her wonderful new vacuum cleaner. She didn't intend to hurt Minnie, she just wanted to give her a surprise that she would never forget.

Gertie had left the vacuum cleaner set up and she bent low over it and whispered,

'Ever clever

Vacuum cleaner,

Ever clever,

Don't be slow!

Ever clever!

Catch that crow!

Ever clever,

Do it well,

Before she knows

I've worked a spell.

Ever clever

Do it quick!

Before she knows

I've worked a trick!'

Gertie flicked the switch of the vacuum cleaner and the black hose snaked out and shot towards Minnie who was just squawking, 'Stupid thing! Stupid thing!' Before she could say it a third time the vacuum in the hose pulled her into its power and sucked Minnie off the windowsill. The long black hose captured her then snaked round in the air twisting and turning in every direction..

Gertie did her best to control the hose. She tried to jump after it but it was moving too quickly. She tried to overpower it with spells but its speedy twisting and turning meant that the spells all missed the target. Two of the spells bounced off the walls and hit the vacuum cleaner at the same time and this had an amazing effect as it suddenly seemed to have extra energy.

The hose flew upwards, it flew down, it whirled Minnie round and round one way then it stopped for a moment before changing direction and whirling and whizzing her the other way.

All this made Minnie cross and frightened at the same time. She squawked and squawked and shouted rude words. 'Hellllllllllllp! Oh hairy bananas! Stopppppppppp! Awk! Oh elephants' ears! Help meeeeeeee! Oh slug's slime! I'm giddy – iddy – iddy – iddy! Rotten apples! Save me, Gertie! Save me!'

But because of all the noise from Minnie and the vacuum cleaner Gertie couldn't hear a word that Minnie was saying. The vacuum cleaner kept on whirling and twirling her in every direction. Sometimes she was only just above the ground and then she was brushing the ceiling. Up and down and round and up and forwards and down and backwards up went the squawking crow. Minnie's feathers were so blustered by everything she looked more like a black feather duster than a bird.

Without warning the vacuum cleaner took on a new and angry tone as it whirred. The sucking became more powerful and gradually Minnie began to disappear into the black snakey hose.

'Heeeeeeeeeeeeeeeeeeeeeellllllllllllllllllllllllllllllllllllp !' wailed Minnie as she vanished down the hose and into the cylinder of the vacuum cleaner. The noise became louder then there was a great loud 'plop!' as Minnie came out of the hose and into the machine. Then there was click. The vacuum cleaner switched itself off and everything was silent.

'Fancy that! I never thought that would happen!' declared Gertie. 'Well, well! What a nice surprise!' There was a smile on Gertie's face.

'Help!' said the hollow voice of Minnie from within the machine. 'I can't get out! It's dark in here and I really hate the dark!'

Gertie picked up the now still hose and shouted down the tube, 'Well, go to sleep then, I should think you need a rest after all that excitement.'

Gertie's voice echoed and boomed around in Minnie's head and she felt most peculiar. She felt even worse a moment later as the vacuum cleaner suddenly switched itself on again whirred into life. Gradually the roar became louder and angrier as it prepared for action. This time it was not sucking it was blowing! Minnie found herself being blown in to the foot of the tube and there she stuck with her beak pointing up the tube and her legs sticking out behind.

The vacuum cleaner did not stop but just kept on blowing and blowing and the pressure behind Minnie built up more and even more until something was bound to happen. Without any idea of what was going on Minnie suddenly felt herself being forced up the tube with tremendous pressure. Faster and faster she went. The black tube snaked across the room again and the nozzle headed straight towards the window. The pressure behind her meant that Minnie was soon travelling faster than a bullet from a gun.

Bang!

With an almighty explosion Minnie was fired from the end of the black tube high up above the garden, above the trees, above the houses and up, up, up and away over the town!

The vacuum cleaner had blasted Minnie with such force that she could not control her flight as she shot over villages, over towns, over rivers and lakes, over woodland and forest and even high over hills and mountains. Minnie gasped for breath because she was going so fast. That was a mistake as the cold air was quite a shock as it hit her insides. After that she learnt to keep her beak shut.

Minnie was going so fast that she began to feel very hot. It became hotter and hotter and the tip of the beak began to glow and Minnie thought she was going to be burnt in flight. A moment later she flew beneath a big black cloud that suddenly began to drop its rain in a heavy down pour. As Minnie flew beneath the cloud the rain drenched her and as the drops hit her beak there were little puffs of steam but she began to feel safer and cooler.

On and on soared Minnie who was squawking meaningless gibberish as she flew. People looked up to see what was making the weird noise but they never found out because Minnie was flying so fast. Further and further she went until eventually she began to slow down. Hardly knowing what she was doing she stretched out her wings and glided down on to a remote mountain in one of the wildest parts of Scotland.

Minnie was over four hundred miles from home. She collapsed on the ground and looked like the end of an old feather duster that someone had thrown away. She didn't know where she was or what she could do and she began to feel quite sorry for herself.

Once Minnie had been shot from her house Gertie collapsed into an armchair. She was totally worn out after so much wild and weird action. Maria jumped up on her lap and purred.

Gertie stroked her and gradually they both relaxed and soon they were fast asleep. After a while Gertie was dreaming. There was a funny knocking sound hammering in her head. 'Knock! Knock! Knock!'

She woke up. The sound wasn't in her head. Someone was knocking on the front door.

'Gertie! Gertie! Are you there?' Bert Hoggings the policeman was at the door.

Gertie was suddenly alert. Had something happened to Minnie? She went to answer the door.

'Hello, Bert. What can I do for you?'

'It's that sign,' said Bert. He was red faced, hot and bothered. 'It's turned nasty again. Says nasty things.'

'Does it? Never mind. Nobody seems to have noticed it. It really doesn't bother me.'

'I've tried to paint it out but the paint won't stick.'

'That's very kind of you, Bert, but don't worry.'

'But it's a nasty thing to have by your house.'

'Do I look like a witch, Bert?'

'Of course you don't.'

'Just leave it then. Now come and have a cup of tea and some cake. You look as though you need something to refresh you.'

'Well, thank you. I don't mind if I do.'

A few weeks went by and Gertie found that life was much more peaceful without Minnie being such horrible a nuisance. After two weeks she also stopped feeling guilty about what had happened and quietly admitted to herself that life had become much easier without her twin sister.

Chapter 9
Minnie Alone

The days and weeks passed and Minnie, still lost in Scotland, gradually recovered some of her spirits. Her main problem was finding the right type of food. Although she was now a crow she really didn't like the food that other crows would eat. Minnie hadn't expected was that she no longer had any magical powers. She couldn't turn a mushroom into a tasty cake or a piece of bark in to a slice of meat.

She learnt that her best chance of finding some proper food was to search for people having a picnic. If she was lucky Minnie would be given a nice ham sandwich or a broken biscuit. She longed for a bacon roll or a cream doughnut but none of the picnickers ever seemed to produce such exciting food.

Much to her surprise Minnie began to miss Gertie rather a lot. Living as a crow in the highlands of Scotland was not much fun for Minnie as there was no-one to talk to. One day some other crows tried to talk to her but she couldn't understand a word that they said. Another thing that she was missing was homemade cakes. Gertie made delicious cakes and even when she was feeling particularly grumpy Minnie was always pleased to visit her twin sister if only to have some tasty cake a proper cup of tea.

Eventually Minnie made a great decision. Somehow she would have to find her way home and then she would visit her sister. As she didn't know where she was Minnie had set herself quite a problem. Eventually she decided to fly as high as she could and see what the land below could tell her. Much to her surprise it told her nothing and so she flew down and settled on a road sign.

'Oh, pickled prunes,' she said to herself, 'what am I to do?'

Minnie sat flapping on the road sign swaying backwards and forwards, clinging on tightly until a huge lorry swept past and with a gust of foul air blew her off and on to the ground.

'Rotten rascals!' she screeched as she lay flapping about in the dust. Strangely, this unpleasant event proved to be a piece of luck as it made Minnie look up at the sign she had been sitting on. The sign said 'Edinburgh and the South' in great big clear letters.

'The south! The south!' Minnie suddenly became excited. 'That's where I want to be,' she shouted but if anyone had been nearby she would not have been heard as at that moment another massive lorry rushed past and blew Minnie over with its ferocious wind.

'Lorries, lorries, lorries! Lousy lorries!' she grumbled. 'I'm getting away from here.' With a flew flaps of her wings she was up in the air above all the foul lorries and flying southwards as hard a she could.

Gradually Minnie worked her way towards her home. She found the flying very tiring and so her progress was slow. She decided following roads and railways was her best plan. Minnie's still could not find the type of food she longed for. She wanted human food and all she could find was an odd scrap of stale bread or an apple core or two.

Flying south, following a big wide road with signs that said M6, Minnie became very tired and so she landed at a motorway service station. Desperate for something tasty she approached a lorry driver who was enjoying a bacon sandwich. The smell of bacon made Minnie feel hungrier than ever and so she hopped as close as she could to the driver.

'Got a bit of bacon?' she asked trying to sound as human as possible. The driver didn't notice her but finished his food and began to check his lorry. Feeling very disappointed Minnie looked up at the lorry and gasped. There was the solution to her problem. On the side of the lorry was the sign 'Pearkins of Worchester' and this made Minnie so excited. 'Worchester! Worchester!' she shrieked to herself. 'I live near Worchester!'

The driver was at one side of the lorry so Minnie hopped round to the back and spying a gap in the vehicle cover she flapped her wings and managed to dive in just before the driver would have spotted her. A few moments later Minnie heard the lorry engine start up and the vehicle began to move. She started to think that she really was on her way back home.

Chapter 10

Minnie Returns

One afternoon, at about teatime, Gertie had her feet resting on a stool. She was sipping some tea and eating hot, buttered crumpets. Suddenly she heard a tapping sound. She looked up and saw a tatty pile of black feathers on the windowsill. The only thing that Gertie recognised was a pair of beady eyes. She went to the window and opened it a little.

'Gertie,' squawked the crow, 'don't you recognise me? It's Minnie!'

'I know it's you, Minnie,' said Gertie, who was able to understand what her sister was saying. 'What do you want?' Gertie was very careful not to open the window too far, as she wasn't going to let Minnie into her house.

'Please help me, Gertie,' Minnie squawked in a very subdued tone. 'I'm in terrible trouble.'

'I'll come outside,' said Gertie. She didn't really want to help Minnie but she thought she should as the sight of her twin sister had stirred some family feelings.

'After all, she is my sister, my twin sister,' Gertie said silently to herself, but she was going to be very careful.

'What do want me to do?' asked Gertie once she was outside. She looked at Minnie and felt quite sorry for her.

'I turned myself into a crow,' said Minnie, 'and I don't know how to turn myself back again!'

'Oh my goodness,' said Gertie. 'That must be nasty.' As she spoke a little smile crept over her face.

'Can you change me back again?'

'No I can't,' said Gertie. 'You are my twin sister and any spell I work upon you will bounce back to me. You'll become human and I'll become a crow. I'm not having that!'

'What ever shall I do?'

'You'll have to stay as a crow, won't you?' said Gertie. 'You'll just have to make the best of it.'

'Can I come and live with you?'

'I'm not having a crow in my house. You can stay in the garden and I'll make sure there's plenty of food for you.'

'Thank you … I think,' said Minnie, but she knew there was nothing else that she could do or say as Gertie was right. Minnie found this rather annoying but she could not think of any solution to her problems.

'And another thing,' added Gertie, 'if you get up to any of your tricks I'll use my vacuum cleaner!'

'Very well,' said Minnie. 'I'll just have to behave and make the most of what I've got.' She was rather quiet and seemed very subdued.

And that's what happened.

Gertie felt happy knowing that she was doing almost the best that she safely could for her twin sister and Minnie actually became a rather nice and well-behaved crow but she never lost the beady gleam in her eyes.

***

A few weeks later Ricky and his mother came to tea with Gertie. It was a lovely day so they sat out in the garden. Whilst they were having tea Minnie kept jumping around them and eating up anything that was dropped.

Since her return she had put on some weight and her feathers had become sleek and tidy.

'That's a very friendly crow,' said Ricky.

'She's well behaved too,' said Ricky's mother. 'She doesn't come too close.'

'Please my I have some cake?' asked Minnie in her squawky voice.

Only Gertie understood her and so she cut a slice of cake, broke it into pieces and put it on the ground for Minnie.

'There you are, Minnie,' she said.

'Minnie,' said Ricky's mother, 'isn't that the name of your sister?'

'Yes it is,' said Gertie, 'my twin sister!' And she smiled happily to herself.

Minnie was eagerly eating the cake and carefully picking up every crumb so that nothing was wasted.

'That's a good crow. Eat it all up,' said Gertie to Minnie.

Minnie glanced up at the sign that was still close to Gertie's home.

'Thank you, Neighbourhood Witch,' squawked Minnie, with a naughty twinkle in her eye.

But Gertie just smiled once more. She was feeling happier than she had been for a long time.